CW01020842

Hello dear stranger!

When an author travels around, they can't help but leave signed copies of their book in their wake. I'm far from touring the world just yet, but please enjoy this signed copy of THE WANDERER, hidden as I wander around Edinburgh for 3 days.

If you have Instagram, don't hesitate to come chat (@MAUDSDRABBLES), I'd love to hear that this copy has been found! :)

- Maud

PS: if you enjoyed this book, feel free to either keep it to yourself or hide and pass it on to a new stranger.

Happy reading

THE WANDERER

Illustration (author's portrait) by Anastasiia Bakhova
Instagram: https://www.instagram.com/jackojpg/

Book covers designed by Maud Lelarge using resources
from Freepik.com: "Knights of the medieval castle" by @liuzishan
(Freepik license: free for personal and commercial purpose with attribution.)

Chapter headers designed using free resources from Canva.com

ISBN: 9798434099660
Independently published with Amazon KDP.

MAUD LELARGE

THE WANDERER

ABOUT THE AUTHOR

Maud is a French graduate who has always had an interest in stories. In high school, becoming a beta-reader for two American writers was an opportunity for her to discover her own love for writing. Now a college student, she dedicates her free time to the dragons, knights and pirates that have taken over her mind. Be careful, however: angst is her favourite thing to write and she loves to collect the tears of her readers.

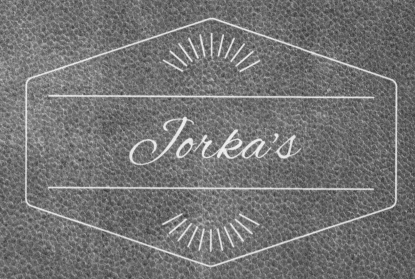

Year XX32

Dear Jorka,

You are only nine, yet I already know you are meant to travel someday. You have this appetite for knowledge, much like your grandfather had. As your mother, I can already tell that the confine of our village won't be enough for you.

When your grandfather tells you stories about the other regions of Zerun and beyond, your eyes shine brighter than they do in front of your favourite meals.

When you decide to follow your dream, I will gift you this notebook, so you can put your first adventures to paper.

I will be waiting for you to tell me your own stories.

With love,

Mom.

THE GUARDIAN OF THE FOREST

LOCATION: THE EMERALD SEA

In the northern part of Zeryn, set between the mountains of the Sleeping Giant and the Valley of Kassera, was the village of Greenblades. Having earned its name from the giant pine trees that grew and towered around the village like a crown, only ever challenged in height by the mountain range behind them, the village of Greenblades was the last stop before crossing the biggest forest of all the land: The Emerald Sea.

Tonight, the village was silent. The moon was high in the sky, sometimes playing hide and seek behind the clouds, sometimes largely visible above the dark silhouettes of the snow-covered mountains. While everyone was expected to be asleep at this late hour, someone had remained awake ever since his parents had tucked him in, waiting for them to go to bed, before he could sneak out of his room. The young boy had patiently waited for the living room's clock to strike midnight, then he'd stepped out of the house as silently as he could, the clicking sound of the closing door covered by the loud, booming noise of the family heirloom clock, legacy of an old ancestor he'd never known but who'd been actively thanking every day for the past month.

Outside, the moon was high in the sky. Though he knew by heart every corner within and beyond the garden walls, the help of the celestial body was not negligible (unless it helped others spot him in the dark, which had almost happened once). After carefully pushing the door behind him, he avoided the muddy pathway and climbed on the garden wall (it wasn't that high, barely a foot tall, and he could easily reach it and jump off of it without hurting himself) so that his footprints wouldn't show in the mud when morning came. Ever so careful, he jumped off the stone wall and landed silently in the high grass behind the house – an area no one cared much about, which worked in his favour for he wouldn't have to make extra efforts to cover his tracks.

The boy came from a family of hunters. He knew the importance of a sharp focus at all times, and he knew that if he wasn't careful, neither his parents nor his big sister would miss the sight of small, fresh footprints in front of the house – ones that definitely should *not* have been there for he should have been fast asleep, and certainly not wandering around on his own in the middle of the night. It wasn't what was expected from a nine-year-old after all: it wasn't safe to be alone at night. Especially where he was heading to.

If his parents knew what he was up to, the boy knew he'd be grounded at home for the rest of his life. His sister would probably scold him as well.

Yet, the thrill of adventure kept him going.

14

In his defence, he was not wandering aimlessly: he was on a mission. Besides, it wasn't the first time he'd snuck out and he had yet to be caught. He was fine. He had everything under control.

Or at least that's what he told himself when, for the tenth time this month he grabbed his carefully packed lantern and lit its small, already half-burned candle, and stepped into the thick forest.

The boy knew it could be dangerous. He knew – having heard all kinds of anecdotes from his dad and the other villagers – how things could turn sour really quickly when you were on your own in the wilderness, even on familiar territory. He knew, yet he was too curious not to go. For the past month, he'd been tracking none other than the Guardian of the Forest and he wanted to see Him.

Coming from the village of Greenblades, the boy had grown up with myths and legends about the Emerald Sea, all inherited from previous generations of storytellers. However, not many people believed in its magic any longer, and while most traditions were forgotten, only childish superstitions spread by strangers across the land subsided. No matter what though, the boy still believed and refused to doubt those stories. A part of them was true, he was sure of it.

When he was younger, his grandfather had told him everything about the magic of the Emerald Sea and he'd told him about the time he saw Him: The Guardian of the Forest.

If the Emerald Sea was home to legendary creatures and the birthplace of many of the Kingdom's legends, the Guardian was its most famous tenant. Few could claim they had seen Him – even fewer spoke the truth about their blessed encounters.

The boy wanted to prove his grandfather was no liar. He would prove to both his parents and his sister that the stories were real and that the Guardian wasn't a mere legend to tell the children around the fire pit. And so, almost every night, the boy slipped out of bed and headed toward the forest in hopes to see Him.

The first time, he'd been scared out of his mind. Scared to be caught, scared to get lost, scared his racing heart would burst in his chest, scared of every little noise that seemed to grow tenfold now that he was surrounded by darkness. Now, he was not so scared anymore. He'd grown used to the sensation, and every trip came with a little more preparation. He had everything he needed in his satchel and more. From snacks to gauze and needles, or even matches and the little pocket knife his father had gifted him on his last birthday, he felt ready to face any situation.

Trusting his feet to lead him to his little observatory, he held onto his candle-lit lantern and walked deeper into the night. Around him, trees looked like dancing shadows, dark leaves shifting to melting gold as he walked by, before disappearing into the night all over again.

As he walked, his hearing was on high alert to make up for the lack of sight. His ears listened to every sound carried within the silence of the night, picking up anything from the shuffling noise of branches around him, the crunching sound of leaves under his feet, or the faraway cry of hooting owls. It was too early in the year to worry about the big predators, he knew that. Yet, it didn't hurt to be a little careful – especially when crossing a forest rumoured to host creatures who didn't all come from the fairy tales that lulled children to sleep.

After nearly an hour's walk, the path cleared, and he released his breath: he'd finally reached the clearing. Above him, the moon was high, basking the nearby trees with a silver glow. The boy smiled at the stars, spotting his favourite constellation with an expert's eye. To see it twinkle above him every night without fault gave him a sense of peace and the courage he needed to come back on his secret explorations. He saw it as his partner in crime, his guide, and his protector.

When he looked down at the ground again, he reached for his satchel. There, carefully tucked between his notebook, his water bottle and his pens, was a cloth-wrapped bowl. Inside, was a mix of black and red berries he'd picked in the afternoon while he'd pretended to go play with the other kids in the wheat fields.

From what his grandfather had told him, they were the Guardian's favourites.

Once he was done arranging his offering in a neat pile at the centre of the clearing (like he had done countless times before), the little boy backtracked toward the forest and headed for his favourite observation spot: an older tree with strong branches, easy to climb even at night, and with foliage thin enough to see past it, yet thick enough not to be seen too easily.

Once he'd settled on his branch, he turned to stone. He didn't move, didn't make a sound. His attention was entirely focused on the centre of the clearing, where he hoped to see the Guardian.

Ever since he'd started to come here, he'd repeated the same ritual: cross the forest, find the clearing, leave an offering for the Guardian, climb the tree, wait for him to show up.

Ever since he'd started to come here, he'd repeated the same ritual, and every time the offering was gone by the time morning came. Yet, the boy had never stayed awake long enough to spot the creature that had taken his gift and whether or not they were the rightful recipient of it.

It didn't help that, no matter if he knew who he was expecting, he didn't know what to look for. In truth, no matter how many stories he'd listened to, the boy didn't know what the Guardian looked like. There were many different legends, each with their own versions – which helped non-believers to think these stories were only old geezers' lies woven together.

The boy knew better than to believe such disheartening truth, however.

"None of those stories are lies," his grandfather had said when the boy had inquired about the confusing tales. "The Guardian simply has different appearances. It's as simple as that."

His grandfather had then argued that he wouldn't be the best Guardian if that weren't the case. He was the safe keeper of their land, and he was able to stay hidden, only choosing to show himself when he deemed souls worthy of encountering Him.

Like most legends, there were different interpretations of those encounters. Some believed it was a good omen to see Him, while others believed the contrary. The boy's grandfather had told him of older traditions, ones older than his grandfather, or the grandfathers that came before him.

In the past, when the Emerald Sea was even bigger than it was now, it was common to send young adults into the forest at night to follow the Guardian's trails. If they were to see Him, depending on the appearance he would take, it held different significations and Elders took it as inspiration to draw information about the children's destiny and what would come in their future. Accepting to go see the Guardian was a test of courage, and when morning came, those who'd been sent – whether they had seen the Guardian or not – were now treated as adults by the other members of the clan.

Whenever his grandfather told him this story, the boy would ask him to tell it over and over again, wanting more details every time, while his sister would sigh and laugh at what she believed were only bedtime stories the old man had invented from scratch. The boy would always frown at that, but no matter what his sister said, she still listened from start to finish, as if some part of her was still interested and was only repeating what she'd heard other grown-ups say.

The boy wanted to prove to her, prove to everyone who didn't believe, that his grandfather was no liar. He would see the Guardian. He would prove them all wrong and make his grandfather proud.

*

It was halfway through the night when the Guardian finally showed.

The mist had started to silently slither between the trees while the temperature had dropped a little, almost making the boy reconsider staying the night, but then... something moved in the darkness across the clearing, startling him.

A beast he'd never seen before, nor in his books nor his dreams, stepped out. Scales as dark as the night covered its body, and even though it was larger and taller than any deer or bear he had already encountered in the forest during hunting trips with his father, this beast made no sound as it stepped onto the grass. It crossed the clearing just as silently, not paying any mind to its surroundings as it walked toward the little mount of berries the boy had left hours prior.

Awestruck, doing his best to hold his breath and not make a single sound, the boy watched as the beast sniffed the offering, reminding the young boy of himself and his sister whenever they came home to the familiar, delicious aroma of their mom's cooking.

When its feast was done, the beast licked the sides of its mouth with its long tongue, as if not wanting to miss a single drop of juice.

Then, it turned around.

Even though he was still hidden by the branches, the boy could tell the beast could see him.

Breath caught in the boy's throat as the beast's eyes bore into his. He kept still, awe shining in his eyes as he met the deep silver orbs of the beast.

There was no doubt now. His grandfather had always told him that one would always know whether he had met the Guardian or not, for, no matter his appearance, his eyes would always stay the same. Akin to the full Silver Moon, they were big and wide and twinkled like stars in the night sky.

The Guardian looked in the boy's direction for what felt like hours but could only have been minutes if not seconds. It held his gaze, and then, as if its curiosity had been satisfied or that it'd determined no threat could come from the small human hiding in the tree, the Guardian looked away. He turned his back to him and put his attention back on the grass at its feet, now berryless.

If the boy didn't know better, he would have argued the Guardian looked sad that he had no more treats to eat.

The Guardian remained in the clearing for a few more seconds after that, enjoying the moonlight and the caress of the late-night mist on its scales. However, before the boy could think about pulling out his notebook, it was gone.

The boy's cheeks hurt from smiling too hard, his chest felt constricted from both too much excitement and holding his breath for too long. Yet, even though he was giddy with happiness, he remained a child who was way past his bedtime and, before he could think of anything else, he fell asleep on his branch.

That night, the boy dreamed about the dragon he had just seen and of the stories he would tell his grandfather the next day.

*

Hours later, when he woke up on his branch, hair in disarray, satchel barely hanging over his shoulder and mind still reeling from his encounter, the sun was already peaking past the mountains. He adjusted his satchel over his shoulder in a hurry, made sure he hadn't forgotten anything and started to cautiously climb down.

However, no amount of precautions could have prepared him for hearing a voice below him.

Startled and caught off guard, his feet slipped on the old and wrinkled bark. Because of the sudden movement, his satchel fell off his shoulder. If it wasn't for his secured grip on a branch he'd caught right on time, he'd have followed his satchel in its fall. Satchel which now sat six feet below, having spilt most of its content at his sister's feet.

"Finally awake?" she asked teasingly, the ghost of a laugh lingering in her tone as she looked up at him. Leaning against the trunk of the tree, it seemed as if she'd been waiting for him for a while.

"What are you doing here," he stuttered, barely recovered from his surprise and already fearing what she had to say, or worse, what she might have already told their parents. "Why aren't you at home?"

She raised an eyebrow at him. "Shouldn't I be the one asking you that question?"

Embarrassed as he'd been caught red-handed, he didn't answer.

While he fixed his nest-like bed hair and rubbed his hands to remove the moss and dirt in his palms, his sister grabbed his satchel on the ground and announced, "I knew you'd been sneaking out."

His hands stopped moving. "You knew?!"

"Of course, I did. I'm your big sister after all. And you're not as

21

sneaky as you think. Who do you think kept mom and dad from going outside too early?" She paused, a tired sigh escaping her lips as she handed him back his satchel. "It's a wonder they didn't find out before I did. You'd be in big trouble otherwise."

"Thank... you?"

"Don't thank me just yet", she warned. "I haven't decided whether I should snitch or not. That was incredibly stupid of you. Dangerous as well. You know you're not supposed to be outside on your own, especially when no one knows where you are."

"But you did," he said, half-smiling, half-wincing – and knowing full well it was a poor attempt at sounding confident and unlikely to work on her if she'd already decided to scold him for his behaviour.

She smacked the back of his head. "You didn't know that. Don't play smart with me."

"Fine," he said, rubbing the back of his head with hands still covered in dirt and scratches from his (almost) fall.

As they walked side by side, she went on rambling about the different dangers of being alone at night in the forest. Yet, after a while, her scolding ran dry, the conversation shifted and he found himself able to tell her about his adventures, choosing to end his tale with his final encounter with the Guardian. He didn't know whether or not she fully believed him, – her sceptical eyes were part of her resting face – yet she listened to him till the end, and only joked a few times that he might have dreamt it all.

They were halfway through discussing the probabilities that it might have really been the Guardian when they reached the end of the forest and stopped in their tracks.

Ahead on the dirt path, with arms crossed over her chest and the twitch of a worried expression on her face, their mother stood, waiting for them both.

The boy stopped, suddenly skittish. Would she be mad?

No, given the look on her face, she *already* was.

He gulped, waiting for *her* scolding this time.

When she didn't move, nor uttered a word, his worry grew worse — his mother's silence was always akin to calm before a storm. Nothing good could come out of it. Already, his brain was trying to come up with a good lie, a good story to tell that she might believe or—

"We went picking berries!" his sister shouted excitedly, taking no time to run toward their mother.

Their mother's frown turned to a confused one. "Berries?"

"Yes, mom. Fresh berries for breakfast, happy birthday!"

Their mother gave her a sideways glance. "My birthday isn't before another week, dear."

"Oh, really? My mistake then," she answered, shrugging at her before turning towards him with an apologetic, almost innocent smile on her face. If it wasn't for the wink she sent him as she spoke, or the big lie that came out of her lips, the boy might have believed it was earnest had he been in his mother's shoes. "Guess I dragged you out of bed for nothing then. My bad."

Then, before their mother could ask anything more, his sister disappeared inside the house, calling for their father, saying breakfast was on the table. Behind him, the boy could still feel the stare of his mother on his back, as if she was still deciding whether to believe or not their story. In the end, if she chose the latter, she didn't show any sign of it and smiled, gently grabbing his hand before entering the house with him by her side.

They ate their breakfast together, something that happened more frequently lately (maybe his sister hadn't lied when she said she'd been keeping their parents inside to cover for him). As he picked a handful of berries to eat with warm bread and a steaming cup of milk, the little boy was already planning his next trip – promising himself that this time, he would not fall asleep.

A stolen glance with his sister made him understand another thing.

Next time, she would come to see the Guardian too.

Year XX40

Today, mom gifted me this notebook. I didn't know what she meant for me to do with it until she told me to fill it with my own adventures.
I'm not going to use these pages yet. I'll leave them to the future, for when I've become the greatest adventurer of Zeryn.

x

Year XX42

I've been accepted! I'm going to the Hereward Academy. I can't believe it. Everyone is beyond ecstatic! This is what I've always dreamed about: I'm going to study the history of those lands and learn everything there is to know about them. Time to chase my dreams!

x

I turned nineteen yesterday. Tomorrow, I'm leaving for Hereward. I cannot wait! I've been waiting forever for this. It'll take a few weeks to reach the city but my time has finally come! First, I'll head east toward the city of Aeldon to join a group of merchants. They're led by a man named Tarel. Mom and dad have met with him before, he'll let me tag along until the end of my journey. Mom says she's never seen me so excited – and just as nervous. I just can't wait!

x

Today is the day. I've said my goodbyes to mom, dad and Ella. Mom said she wouldn't cry, but obviously she failed. Even dad got a bit emotional before I left. I'm already homesick at the thought of leaving them, grandpa, and everything I've ever known for so long. Yet, at the same time, I'm excited about the travel that awaits me. My very first adventure!

x

Dear Jorka,

As your mother, I am sad to see you go. I wish I was able to keep you close all my life, however, I know this is not what you need. This is why, as your mother, I am proud to see you chase your dreams. I am happy for you. I know you have been waiting for this since you were born and I know you will do great. You are about to embark on a journey you will remember for the rest of your life. I hope it will be even better than what you imagined.

Please, don't forget to send us letters, you know I will worry too much otherwise. Make good use of your notebooks and write down everything, so you don't forget any details in the stories you'll tell me and the others. After all, how can I brag about my son, if I don't know what he's up to?

I love you, my little Jorka.

May the stars protect you on your travels.

Mom.

Safe travels, son. Make us proud! — Dad.

Don't do anything stupid. I will know and
I'll come to kick your ass - Ella
PS: don't forget to send me souvenirs.

Your sister sounds fun Jo!
— Jack

> travel boots
> extra shirt
> grandpa's compass
> pen sharpener
> notebook
> money to pay Tarel
> sandwich

After travelling in a cart for six hours, I finally reached Aeldon. Unlike Greenblades and its decreasing amount of inhabitants, the housing districts built around the Fort of Aeldon grow in numbers every year. Every time I come here, it feels like the city has grown bigger.

x

I found Tarel and his men waiting by the city's gates and gave him mom's coins. Tarel is relatively intimidating. He's broader and taller than dad, but he welcomed me right away. Other travellers will be on the road with us. Mostly merchants and craftsmen but I've also seen a family who'll accompany us. We'll depart in two days.

x

Today, Tarel has given me instructions and an address to buy myself better travel boots. Even though I'll be riding horseback, according to him, my current soles are too thin for the travel that awaits. I'm the only one accompanying him and his men all the way to Hereward so far. Others will join on the way though.

x

Tonight, I'll spend my last night at the inn.
Tomorrow, the true adventure will start.

x

Today, as we got ready to depart, Tarel and his men swore to protect us and guide us to each of our destinations. Some part of me wishes everything will go according to plan, safe and without risk. The part of me that longs for adventures though, thinks it would make a good story if it didn't. After all, I'm quite curious about the scars Tarel's skin bears and I wonder if the axe on his back is only decorum...

x

It's not, trust me on this. You do not want to be his opponent. - Jack

Is it weird that I haven't yet fully realised everything that is happening? I'm going to become a student at the Academy. I'm following my dream. It all feels surreal still. (My painful limbs, however? Very aware of them, thank you. Who knew riding for hours could hurt like this?)

x

The landscape has already changed a lot since I've left. The terrain is much easier to cross here, less steep, with different species of trees than the pine forest I'm used to and way more room for crops and cattle. The only thing that doesn't change is the mountains. Day after day, they get smaller in the distance, yet their silhouettes are still towering over everything. It's quite impressive, and comforting as well. It still feels like I have a bit of home with me, whenever I look at them.

The other night, Tarel joked we can see the mountains even from the other side of the continent. I think that because I told him I want to become a storyteller, he takes me for a bit of a fool. I'm not a fool, I'm a dreamer - there's a difference. Whenever I tell him that though, he laughs and taps me on my shoulder like I've seen him do when he and his men joke around a pint at the tavern.

I've learned to no longer take offence in that. That, or I've gotten greedy for the stories that are stored in his mind. After so many years spent on the road and the seas, he has so much to say. Dad was right: Tarel is no ordinary merchant. He seems to know every corner of the land and he even fought with pirates! I wonder if we'll meet pirates on the way to Hereward... (Mom would have an aneurysm if she could read this.)

x

To pass the time, whenever I'm not helping others, I think about stories in my head. I wonder about the events the century-old trees we pass by have seen, I dream about the viewpoint of the birds that fly over us, and whenever anyone shares their story around the fire pit at night, I imagine what it was like, even though I've never been to the lands they describe. Maybe one day. For now, dreams are all I have to travel beyond all borders. Every night, I fall asleep thinking about the day the roles will swap and I'll be the one telling my stories.

THE EMERALD SEA

The Emerald Sea is dark and thick with trees, its fog heavy with legends and unsolved mysteries. According to bedtime stories, if you are brave enough to follow the path amongst its white flowers and blades of grass, the trail will guide you to a secret and foreign land, home to legendary magical creatures.

Some folks believe the area is to be feared, haunted by the ghosts of a past only trees can remember. Others worship the forest like they would a god, while some, oblivious to the tales, walk by without ever seeing the magic contained in its leaves.

THE RIVER'S SECRET

As the blooming warmth of Spring melted the glaciers, crystal water began to trickle down the mountain. Sometimes loud as a roar, sometimes soft as a whisper, it stubbornly forced its way past polished rocks, slithered between century-old trees, washed away driftwood and fallen blooms, before ending its race in the open arms of the valley below.

Unforgiven as it seemed, the pulsing river hid a well-kept secret. And if one were to listen carefully, they would hear the giggles of sunbathing fairies and the whispered pranks of mischievous goblins, mixing with the gurgles of the river they called home.

BEFORE YOU GO

The old priestess stepped into the woods, nostalgia squeezing her heart. Seven decades ago, when her apprenticeship had ended, she'd come here with the other students to celebrate. Now passing by the same towering oak trees, she couldn't help but ache for the joy she'd felt that day. Nothing was the same now.

When she reached the clearing, the big, obsidian eyes of the sleeping dragon opened weakly to observe her.

Tears welled in the corner of her eyes.

Soft, wrinkled hands met sharp, iridescent scales.

An hour later, the last living dragon released its final breath in her embrace.

ETERNAL WITNESS

In the bright and blinding ocean of white, a tall, imposing shadow stood on the horizon. The black silhouette belonged to an old castle. The wind had long replaced the residents. Now, only shards of broken glass and clouds of dust danced in the halls.

People had forgotten the story behind the ruins, the face of the duke who once lived there and the laughter of the children in the halls.

There, in this desolate landscape, a single rose bloomed in the gardens, bleeding through the black and white canvas. Sole witness to the castle's legacy, it would never wither.

I'm counting down the days since I left Greenblades. I can't wait to reach Hereward. I wonder if the city is as amazing as Tarel has described it to be.

x

My horse's name is Zephyr. I thought she didn't like apples, because she always refused the ones I offered her. Today, however, I was eating one next to her and she stole half of it from me. Turns out, she only likes the green ones. And only if they've been cut before. That, or she loves to steal what's mine. Did Ella put a spell on her? Zephyr's picky eater habits already reminded me of her but now she's a prankster just like her. This is going to be a long trip.

x

It's been three days since we left Aeldon. Since then I've started to get to know more about Tarel's men. Few are around my age, most of the people who travel with him are closer to their fortieth birthday than their nineteenth. I don't mind, though. It means they have even more stories to tell. As for the cook, he too has spent many years on the road. Every day he cooks us something different, even with the little supplies that we have. The little girl from the family travelling with us calls him the Magician. Even though it started as a joke, I think the new nickname is going to stick amongst the crew.

x

From afar, Tarel can look a bit scary. He's strong and sometimes has the manners of a gruff lumberjack who got up on the wrong side of the bed, but he's actually really nice. He and his men have been on the road together for years now. Every other traveller can tell they trust each other with their life. When I look at them, they remind me of the family I left behind in Greenblades. Sometimes, they prank each other the way Ella and I would do. (Never on duty though, Tarel has too much authority for them to go against his orders - though Tarel is not one to say no to pranks either. Travelling with them sure is lively!)

x

We'll reach the outskirts of Beryl in two days. I'm excited. Soon, we'll reach the harbour, and the next part of our travel will start. Tarel had left some of his men in town (something about unfinished business). One of them is only a year older than me and Tarel expects us to get along. He told me we share the same interest in travels and adventures.

x

Because I'm the best !

We're staying in Beryl for the week. Tarel has deals to make and more passengers to wait for. The crew he hired to take us to Hereward by the sea will arrive in five days. The cook is placing bets: "Will young Jorka be seasick?" is their new favourite topic of discussion. Torel pretends to be on my side - as if he isn't the one who started the whole thing. Traitor.

x

Since we arrived in Beryl, we've been staying at a tavern close to the port. Every night, I end up staying too late, listening to the stories of those sailors who seem to have lived dozens of lives on the sea. I don't know if half of those stories are all true, but the innkeeper's daughter told me to pretend they are. "Whom does it hurt to dream?" is what she told me when I asked her if she believed all that they said to her. I like the spirit. Every night, I keep asking them questions, and the both of us get to hear more stories - and she gets more coins for all the extra pints they drink. All in all? It's a win-win situation for both of us.

At least they're better off with my questions: the other night, Tarel's men played poker against a few sailors. They lost. Then they decided to play to win back their money. Lost again. Whoops.

Shut up, Jo.

x

I think I'll write a story inspired by the people I've met here. I've already written a few things down here and there. Izzy (the innkeeper's daughter) asked me about what I was writing the other night and I let her read what I'd started. She told me to mail them to her once I'm done. She said she was excited to read the next part. Must admit it's a nice feeling to be able to share my stories with someone.

x

ACROSS THE SEVEN SEAS

LOCATION: HARBOUR TOWN OF BERYL

Lucky sat on the pontoon, letting her feet dangle above the water. It was still early in the morning and the town was barely starting to wake up. The port, however, was already buzzing with life. On the horizon, frigates, topsail schooners and other full-rigged ships, each more amazing than the last, kept appearing and disappearing into the morning fog. Some of them were coming home, their hold probably filled to the brim with the treasures of their adventures; but most of the ships, in full sail, were set for the open sea, heading to countries Lucky could only dream of and visit in her sleep.

One day, she thought. One day it'd be her turn. One day she'd be the hero of the stories the mariners told every night as she poured them "one last" ale.

No matter if those drunk sailors exaggerated their stories or not, Lucky would never get tired of them, there was something about those stories that drew Lucky toward them. But how couldn't she feel this way when hearing the tales of foreign lands, of the creatures that lived in the ocean, of the calm sea turning to a shipwrecking trap as pyramidal waves hit the hull, becoming strong opponents to even the fiercest navigators.

All sorts of people visited the tavern. If sailors were most common amongst her regulars given the proximity of the establishment to the port, it wasn't rare for Lucky to serve travelling merchants who'd stopped for the night, town guards during their break, or even itinerary performers: comedians, musicians, dancers, sometimes fortune-tellers, stepped on the dim-lit wooden stage at the back of the room, hoping to earn a few coins by entertaining the crowd of drunk patrons. If not all of them were blessed with talent, they did break the monotony and Lucky had noticed the mood was often lighter during the nights they attended.

Among all the people that came to the tavern, Lucky loved artists the most. Whenever they were there, charcoal sketches drawn all over the yellowed pages of their notebooks, it felt as if she could travel through the pictures, as if she could feel the salty breeze of the sea, the dry heat of the land they were describing, see the curious animals they had witnessed or the beautiful people they had encountered. Once, one of the men had gifted her one of his drawings and to this day, it was one of her most treasured possessions. A secret too. No one could know what really went through her mind. No one could know how much she yearned to be standing on the deck of a ship, the wind rushing in the sails above her head. She dreamed of such freedom at night, of the adventures she could have travelling across the seven seas…

No. No one could know, especially not the Thenards. Madame

would give her a good lesson if she were to speak such thoughts in front of them. They didn't want her to think about such things, didn't want her to think about anything else but her tasks.

Cleaning dishes, tables and bedsheets, *this* was Lucky's daily life. No thrilling adventures.

Lucky had been working for the Thenards for as long as she could remember. They owned one of the many taverns in town and had been there for decades already, the Thenard's parents before them. Madame Thenard had taken over after her parents passed away.

She was the one in charge. That's what she always said.

That, and the fact that she'd been the one to save Lucky, that the young woman should be grateful for that, that she needed to own her keep now that she was old enough to work.

"You're lucky you have a roof over your head, girl," Madame would say with her disagreeable hoarse voice, *"Not everyone is that lucky these days. We give you food. We never hurt you. Just asking for a little help around the house in return. You're a lucky girl."*

Lucky.

Madame claimed it so often that it had become her name. She hated it. There was nothing lucky about being treated like a slave, for not being beaten up or raped when such treatments should never be a thing.

Those thoughts, Lucky kept for herself too. It seemed men weren't fond of that independent spirit of hers – and neither were the Thenards.

So Lucky kept her secrets to herself and hid the drawing in the seams of her dress, hummed sailor songs to herself as she cleaned the dishes and imagined the big, white sails of a full-rigged ship as the wind was caught in the drying bedsheets.

One day, Lucky. One day, it'll be your turn. One day…

But for now, it was time for her to head back if she didn't want the Thenards to start questioning her whereabouts. She'd been out for an hour already and if she didn't come back with the groceries soon, Lucky wasn't sure Madame would keep her fists to herself this time.

Jumping to her feet, she grabbed the huge basket next to her and heaved it in her arms. Tonight, Madame was making a big stew and wanted all the ingredients ready for the fine navy boats that would soon arrive in town, with tons of wealthy soldiers aboard.

Lucky doubted they would even set foot in their poor looking tavern but once again, Lucky had kept her thoughts to herself, had taken the few coins Madame had handed her and had headed straight away for the market plaza before allowing herself a few minutes of rest.

A commotion coming from down the street caught Lucky's attention. Just like many merchants around her, she turned her head toward the noise, trying to figure out what was going on.

The sound of boots against the cobbles, the recognizable sound of swords coming out of their sheaths and dozens of shouting voices. Men – no, soldiers – came rushing around the corner, chasing after a man who was wearing a *way too happy* grin for someone who was being chased by the guardsmen. They didn't hold the reputation of being the kindest people in Zeryn.

If Lucky had seen the rushing man, he didn't seem to have seen her and bumped into her at full speed as he turned around to mock the soldiers. It sent her basket rolling on the side, bread and fresh vegetables tumbling down the streets, orphans' grabby hands already taking them away.

Madame was not going to be happy about that.

Before she could speak her mind to the stranger, however, he grabbed her by the arm and started to drag her along with him.

"Let go of me!" she shrieked but it only deepened his grin before he turned around and rushed into a dark alleyway, never slowing his pace.

Lucky had no idea where he was leading her, never letting go of her arm as he took yet another shortcut that led them back to the port.

But it's a dead-end, Lucky's mind protested.

There was nothing toward this part of town apart from drunk men and beggars who often failed to see the edge and ended up tumbling down into the sea, their bodies never to be seen again.

Lucky and any other human endowed with a brain would avoid this district.

The young woman had no idea where the stranger was going, didn't want to know — and didn't want anything to do with it! All she could think about was Madame's wrath when she'd see she wasn't back. And even if she would, Lucky would come home late and empty-handed. She didn't have any coin left to buy once more any of the goods Madame had asked for — the ones the stranger had ruined for her.

Then, with a sharp halt of her heart and a strangled breath, Lucky realised where they were heading and she didn't like any of it. Not only had a stranger — who was being chased by the army — kidnapped her but he also happened to be crazy. Even crazier than she had first expected him to be. No sane man would be running at such speed to a freaking dead-end that had killed so many people in the past. No sane man would be running at such speed if they didn't actually plan to-

Crap.

He actually planned to do just that.

He was going to freaking jump off the cliff and had all the intention to drag her along with him!

Lucky tried to stop him, cursing after her frail build that made it easier for him to take her with him no matter if she tried to fight him or not.

The stranger let go of her hand, but before Lucky could taste the satisfaction of victory, his arm looped around her waist.

"Hold on tight!", he shouted, having the audacity to smile at a time like this.

Lucky's eyes widened as his free hand grabbed one of the ropes that hung from one of the house's pulleys, all while continuing to run straight for the cliff.

These small pulleys had been used in the past to take away the cargo from the bigger ships that were docked below, but now that the new port had been built on the other side of the city, well more designed and with better equipment, they didn't need them anymore.

What was this man actually planning to do?!

A scream tore through her throat as he held onto the rope and jumped over the edge.

She closed her eyes and in a final prayer to a god she had ignored all her life, waited for her final moment to come.

When the cold freezing water didn't swallow her whole and she didn't feel any different than she had been a few minutes before except for a racing heart and a confused brain, she willed herself to open her eyes, ready to tear apart the man's throat for what he had done to her.

This wasn't at all what she wanted when she said she wanted an adventure. Yes, she wanted to escape that dreadful life but kidnapping hadn't been part of her existing plan. What had that stranger been thinking?! Not that she actually thought the man was capable of reason as he had been the one running from the guard and jumping straight to the end of the street only to land on—

Where was she exactly, anyways?

The sunlight blinded her when she opened her eyes to try and answer her own question.

Her vision was out of focus, her heart threatened to burst in her chest and as for her breathing, it had yet to come back to its regular pattern after such a run and commotion of emotions.

It took a few more seconds for all three to settle and go back to a semblance of normalcy.

She wasn't dead – that one was obvious. Her broken body wasn't laying at the bottom of the ocean; she could feel the heat of the sun on her skin. She wasn't underwater. Plus, even if her breathing was still a little erratic, she could breathe just fine.

But then, what was the hard floor she could feel under back?

Because there was no way she was laying on the deck of a ship after surviving such a fall and that a dozen figures were staring down at her – right?

It was all her imagination.

She had probably dozed off on the pontoon and she was going to wake up any time soon.

"She lives!" someone with a rough accent shouted, extending his hand so Lucky would get up.

She refused and jerked to her feet, her legs nearly collapsing under her as she stood back up.

Lucky was definitely awake and she didn't know what was supposed to be worse: the fact that it meant that everything that had happened was real and that she was in deep trouble when Madame would come for her; or the fact that she had obviously been captured by some random rogues? If they expected to use her to escape the army or get some ransom, then they'd definitely be disappointed.

"Who are you?!" Lucky reached for the knife she kept in her belt and cursed when she didn't find it. It had either fallen in the tumult or they had taken it away from her. "What do you want with me?"

"Good question." The sailor tilted his head, eyeing her with a suspicious glare. Much like the rest of the crew, his skin was tanned from a life at sea, working under the sun. He had a slight accent that slurred some of his words, one similar to a sailor's she'd met at the tavern who came from the northern borders of Zeryn, beyond the mountains of the Sleeping Giant. "What are you doing on our ship!?"

He was kidding, right?

"Some crazy bastard abducted me and brought me here, that's what I'm doing!"

The man turned to the stranger from the port, a big desperate sigh escaping his lips. "Really, Captain? You did it again?"

Now that Lucky actually had the time to acknowledge her kidnapper, she stared at his outfit which was way too nice and pretty for someone who lived at sea. It didn't seem to be a navy officer uniform either – none of the sailors wore any. The black, embroidered coat reached his knees, covering dark pants and a loose white shirt. A feathered hat, just as casual and discreet as his coat, hid his features. A big smile spread across his face at his crewmate's comment.

Captain, huh?

"Oh come on, Lachlan, what would be the fun of halts if I didn't spice things up?"

"We would have a good rest for once, without having to run away from yet another town guard."

44

"Like I said, not funny."

Lachlan rolled his eyes at that and pointed at Lucky. "And what are we supposed to do with that, now?"

"Oh, I don't know. First of all, stop speaking like this, you're being rude to our guest." The captain turned back to Lucky, removing his hat as he did so, and letting long and somewhat familiar brown locks fall back on his shoulder. "What's your name, honey?"

Her. Lucky realised, correcting herself as the captain set his playful eyes on her again. The captain was a *she*! And Lucky realised upon meeting her eyes, that she was no stranger at all.

"What do you mean, what's your name?" Lachlan interrupted, a frown on his face, "You don't know her!? You dragged yet again another person into this mess and you don't know her?!"

The captain shrugged, smiling innocently.

"I know you," Lucky said bewilderedly, everyone's attention turning to her. "I saw you at the tavern the other day. You were dressed as a fortune-teller."

"Sure did, sweetheart~"

The captain had been wearing a dress at the time, Lucky remembered. With a green corset and her long hair curling on her shoulder, golden trinkets pinned over them. The sailors had been obsessed with her that night and hadn't told her many stories. They were too curious to know about their great future, too distracted by her pretty looks to pay attention to Lucky any longer.

But the fortune-teller had come to her afterwards, when all the men were gone and the Thenards were already upstairs, sleeping soundly. She had taken Lucky's hands, fake golden bracelets tingling at her wrists and even if Lucky had tried to explain to her that she didn't believe in any of those things, the fortune-teller had predicted her future anyways.

"Soon," the woman had said, *"Soon your life will take a new turn and it'll be up to you to take that opportunity."*

Her words had been so strange that they had stuck in her mind. Silly, too. There was no way her life would change. No matter how much she longed and ached for it, Lucky knew it was wishful thinking to hope someday an adventure would come knocking at her door.

The captain folded her arms over her chest and looked at Lucky with a knowing smile as if she knew Lucky was recalling the words she had told her that night.

Lucky took a step back, gauging the captain and her crew with confused eyes. She didn't know when the sails had been lowered but the port was already far away from them.

"The guard won't be able to follow us here, it's not worth the trouble for them. Lazy bastards, those soldiers." The heels of the captain's knee-high leather boots clicked against the wooden deck as she closed the gap between them. Her liquor-coloured eyes bore into Lucky's as she whispered, "So what do you say, huh? Wanna escape that dreadful life of yours and go on an adventure?"

"You want to welcome someone you don't even know aboard?" Lachlan shouted again. "What's bloody wrong with you?"

"I didn't know you either," the captain argued. "We're all strangers to someone at some point, didn't keep any of us from becoming friends. Plus, I didn't say I didn't know her, just that I didn't know her name."

Except she did. She had whispered it on her way out of the tavern the other day. With how many times Madame growled her name every hour, it was no surprise that she had heard it. The captain didn't seem to be the kind of person who forgot anything.

Lucky took another quick look around her, stared at the gigantic sails, at the people buzzing to their own task, at the ocean surrounding her, at the town getting tinier and tinier with every minute that went by.

"What's your name, my friend?" The captain asked again, a warm smile across her face.

If she already knew her name, then why did she keep on asking?

"Soon your life will take a new turn and it'll be up to you to take that opportunity."

Lucky smiled, finally understanding.

A new name.

A new name for a new life, that's what it was all about.

As she took a second to answer, she recalled her favourite hiding spot on the rooftop of the tavern, covered in ivy roots that grew and managed to escape, away from the tavern. How many times had she almost felt envious of the green roots and leaves, living and growing everywhere they wanted? Now it was her time to choose her path and leave the gloomy walls of the prison the tavern represented for her.

"Ivy," she finally replied, "You can call me Ivy."

The captain reached out her arm to shake hands, "And I am Aega, Captain of the Sea Dragon. Welcome aboard my ship, Ivy."

Ivy smiled in response and took the captain's hand.

Today, her new life was starting.

Ports are loud. Much louder than I thought they'd be. Everywhere I look, there's always someone running, shouting orders, cursing after something, running again. And that's on forgetting the seagulls screeching above us all, trying to steal anything they can. Ports are loud, smelly, confusing and all those things that should make me hate the whole experience after growing up in the peaceful silence of Greenblades and the smell of pinewood in the air. And yet, it was the most fun I had in weeks. Tarel and his men know all kinds of places and people, there's always something to do, someone to see, I love it!

x

I hadn't connected the dots yet but taking the sea means leaving Zephyr behind. It's easier to pay for other horses when we reach the coast again. Who would have guessed I'd get attached to this i-eat-your-apples-only traitor of a horse?

x

The sight of ships caught in the morning fog is almost as mystical as the forest vanishing in the mist back home. There's something eerie about their shadows disappearing in this thick, white blanket. Suddenly, it seems all the noise from the harbour comes from nowhere.

x

It's almost been two weeks since I left home. Today, new people are joining our group to travel with us. Tarel is to guide them to the eastern coast. We'll cross their town on our way to the capital (our next and final meeting point before we reach Hereward) and we'll part ways there.

x

We leave tomorrow. Time to finally find out how well I'll handle this next part of the waves. I don't want to be sick... Our captain is hopeful, though: the wind should be good and the worst storms of the seasons are behind us already. Let's hope he is right.

x

Hello Jorka! It's Jack!

Stole your notebook for the day. You've been sick since we left. Don't worry, you'll get used to the waves soon enough. In the meantime... the mighty Jack will take care of your writing logs.

What do you even write in those anyways? (No, I'm not a bad friend, I didn't skim through your things. Okay, I did take the notebook but it's for a good cause! I'm recording in your stead. Doubt your descendants will want to know more about the meal you're throwing up right now. Right?

We've departed from Beryl two days ago. Slightly offended that you didn't mention my name before that. I thought we were friends, Jo. J&J! The best of friends, come on! (Did I mention that I didn't read anything? Okay maybe I lied. Just a little. The stories are good though! Izzy didn't lie about that fact.)

Onboard the Demarion, there are about a dozen crew members and twice the amount of passengers (mostly from our group, though). If Tarel seems to know every road, the captain of the Demarion is just as smart when it comes to sea currents. Once you recover, I'm sure he can tell you many stories. Maybe he'll teach you how to read a marine map, they look nothing like the maps I know. Forget about the roads and small pathways like the one drawn on Tarel's detailed scrolls. Here, it's rows upon rows of marine routes, safe ports to drop anchor, dangerous pathways or even previous pirate encounters! Can you believe it?

The sea is beautiful. It's all around us and looks like oil when the sun rises or sets. You've yet to see it for yourself but I'm sure that once you recover and adjust to the sea, you'll love the scenery. And at night? It's pure blackness like you've never seen before. No one around us. No sound but the ones of the waves hitting the hull and the occasional chats of the sailors exchanging shifts.

According to the captain, you'll feel better in the morning. Here, your notebook is back in your pack. You won't even notice it was gone (unless you see my entries of course, which I don't doubt you will). Have fun witnessing all this for yourself, Jo!

I am alive again. Finally, I was tired of being sick. The fact the vessel's rolling doesn't stop when you're in bed - because we all sleep in hammocks - doesn't help. Both the captain and Tarel assured me I'm better off this way. If I had a real bed, I'd keep moving around and it'd be worse.

Another thing: Jack stole my notebook last night and left a few notes to make up for my absence. Now he's looking at me with big eyes as I write because he's still offended I didn't talk more about him until now. So let's hear it: Jack is the youngest of Tarel's men, only a year older than I am. He wants to become a cartographer and has been travelling with Tarel since he was fourteen. It's not his first time on the sea. He's also a cheater and a traitor: much like the others, he hasn't stopped teasing me about my past sickness. I'm much better now, though. Ready to face the sea and annoy people with my questions all over again!

x

When sailing, it's important to stay hydrated to avoid sunstroke and to eat fruits to avoid sickness. We only left a few days ago and the trip won't last months (only a couple of days if the weather is merciful) so the hull is still full of fresh groceries. However, while we're at sea, the Magician is no longer in charge of our meals. It could be because I'm still feeling a little unwell, but I can't say Demarion's cook is as great as ours...

x

Now that I get to spend my nights with the crew again, I get to hear everyone's story. I've heard most of Tarel's men's past already but now I get to know more about the sailors we're travelling with. Most of them have joined the crew long ago and are fully devoted to their captain. They often joke that the thing they love most about him is that he pays them well and allows them a two-day rest in every port (which they translate to 'two days to get drunk before getting back to work': a true sailor's way.)

When they're not drunk, the sailors teach me many things about the ship, from the names of the sails to the wonders of navigation. My favourite part is when they tell me about the legends of the sea: mythical creatures, travel anecdotes & historical events all mix together in a one of a kind tale!

x

Remember when the captain said we wouldn't get a storm? Yeah, well. Lies and slander! I spent yesterday locked away in the quarters with the other passengers. Sick, all over again. With roll and pitch motions worse than ever before. Only crewmates were allowed on deck to avoid any accidents, so even Tarel and his men were there with us. They kept us distracted with their stories and reassuring words of: "Come on, it's only a little wind", "we've survived worse than this", "one time, the mast broke and we had to fix the sails in the middle of a bloody typhoon!" Do you see the irony? I felt far worse after listening to them than I did when all my attention was focused on the wind howling above us. Tarel's men aren't really good at saying the right thing to avoid stress.

For now, however, the storm is behind us! We've stayed on course, so the worst has been avoided, or so the captain said. I sure hope we won't face another storm, it's official: I'm meant to stay on land. One day, maybe, I'll wake up with sea legs. This day isn't here yet, though.

We've already established that I hate storms, that's a given now. However, when the wrath of the sea stops, it's just as Jack said. It's beautiful and breathtaking to see the ocean as far as our eye can see; a little disorientating as well. But still pretty. I'm impressed that Jack can say at all times where we are: even during the day, he's able to calculate the position of the stars and tell me in which direction we're heading. Every night, I try to spot the constellation of the Wanderer. Even after all these years, it still accompanies me on every adventure. I wonder if Ella looks up at the night sky at times and remembers our numerous (not so secret) excursions under its protection.

To celebrate the passing of the storm, we're all partying tonight (not that parties aren't happening every other night, but this time there's an official excuse). I already knew (from observing them in Beryl and from the stereotypes that precede their arrival) that sailors know how to party and hold their liquor. It's no less true when they're at sea, it seems. They drink until late into the night and sing loudly under the stars. I'm starting to learn the lyrics of some of the shanties, but their repertoire is so big, that I learn a new one every day. Jack always has one stuck in his head, and he keeps singing them from sunrise to sunset.

THE SIREN'S CALL

The boat sways gently.

On-board, sailors sing shanties as they complete their tasks. There is no storm in sight, not a single cloud on the horizon. Nothing but blue skies, warm sunlight and the vast open sea.

Oblivious to the threat that lurks beneath, they pay no mind to the slight change in the wind and the smell of seaweed it carries. When the first notes fill the air, not a single one of them resists Their tempting melodies.

Within minutes, air and sea currents become sole masters of the vessel.

Sailors are lost at sea.

The boat sways silently.

CALM BEFORE THE STORM

Tarel stood amongst the riggings of the ship, watching the horizon from his spot in the crow's nest. So far, there was nothing to report. The weather was sparing them for the first time in weeks and both the sky and sea were clear. Everything was peaceful.

He should have known it wouldn't last.

Minutes later, a shadow appeared to starboard: tall, fast and heading straight toward them.

Without wasting time, Tarel took out his spying glass. Dread filled his veins as he caught sight of the approaching ship's flag.

There, flying in the morning wind, was the black flag.

CHILDREN OF THE ISLE

Bedtime stories warn children about the witches in the woods who eat the misbehaved ones. But who warns witches about the monsters lurking in their own shadows? No one.

And tonight, another has fallen.

But what could she have done, alone and powerless, against five of those monsters? After all, witches aren't used to playing the part of the prey.

Sole witness to the scene, a lonesome raven is the only one able to spread the tale. However, few are the witches willing to believe the story of the Isle of Karmeda – where children are the ones eating witches for breakfast.

ASHES & RUINS

On the seventh day of the Silver Era, the mountain woke from its century-old slumber. Birds had long fled their nests and humans their homes when Earth rumbled, tearing streets and walls apart as easily as paper sheets.

A deafening explosion echoed on the island, choking the sounds of waves before a sky-scraping column of ash and fire burst through the sky, clouding the sunlight. As ashes fell back on earth soundlessly, racing rivers of raging lava hurtled down the flanks of the mountain.

When the destructive flow reached the shores, nothing was left but melted craters and petrified ruins.

Aside from the storm, there are other things that are less fun when sailing. Less fun at best, discouraging at worst. Let's take cleaning, for example. Every time the crew cleans the deck, you can be sure a wave will wash away all their hard work. Then, there's also the work of the woodworker. There's always something to fix on the ship. Sails also need to be mended and checked as well, without forgetting the rigging - especially after a storm when everything has been a little roughed up.

x

Jack's favourites crewmembers onboard are not humans: it's the cats. Onboard the Demarion, there are three of them. They all have different personalities, and while you see the red one most often, the white one is less seen on deck when everyone is milling about. Jack became best friends with the black one, he follows him around all the time (I suspect it's because Jack cheats and gives him food all the time) and Jack argues it was meant to be. He asks for the cat to come with him for good luck when the crew is playing card games together.

x

The weather changes all the time and so quickly when we're at sea. It never stays the same and one has to stay vigilant at all times. That's what the captain said and he always boasts that it is his favourite part of sailing: both the weather and the sea keep him on his toes at all times and though he can predict their moves, they sometimes manage to throw him off and surprise him. Today, no storm in sight. Or rather: nothing in sight. The fog is so thick we can barely see anything past us. We're travelling more slowly for safety, but the captain told me the fog is a good sign. It means we're getting closer to our destination.

x

Whales! We saw whales! We'd seen dolphins the other day, and fish that fly above water as well. The ocean is wonderful. To think an entirely new world hides underneath the surface...

x

After ten days at sea, the land is back. At first, only a thin line on the horizon, the coast grew bigger as we sailed closer, carried by the morning wind that seemed almost as impatient as us.

x

I understand now, why the eastern coast earned its nickname. The chalk cliffs of the Pearl Coast are bright and white, basked in the comforting sunlight that welcomes us on the other side of the Kingdom. As we sail closer to shore, I can't help but think of the dark cliffs that witnessed my departure only weeks ago, on the other side of the country. It feels a little weird to remind myself that home is on the opposite side of where I stand now. Yet, the tingling excitement of new adventures and explorations to come erases my homesickness. We haven't docked yet, and already my mind is reeling. The shouts and yells coming from the port remind me of Beryl and the last few nights we spent before we sailed with the Demarion crew. I'll miss them, just as I'll miss the others when the time comes to say goodbye to Tarel, Jack and everyone else.

However, it isn't time for goodbyes yet and one has decided not to leave us at all. Black is still sitting on Jack's shoulders as if he belongs there and always has. I wonder if the stray will follow him away from the ship.

x

Captain vs Jack: one believes his new best friend will follow him everywhere, while the other who's known Black since he was a kitten is persuaded the cat is no treacherous furball. The bets are on. (I'd be called a traitor if I wasn't on Jack's side, yet... I have my doubts...)

x

The harbour we dock in is about the same size as Beryl. With men and boats coming and going everywhere I look. We won't stay long: we're going straight to the capital. For this part of the travel, it seems I'm still not getting rid of ships: because the city of Zeryn is crossed by the river, we'll be travelling on a narrowboat.

x

Jack lost. He almost won, but he lost. As we were about to leave town, Black jumped off his shoulders and left us, meowing in our direction as if to say goodbye now that we had reached our destination. As I watched him leave, there was no doubt in my mind that he would find his way back to the captain's shadows, his rightful home. At that moment, we all realised Black had been watching over us and on the captain's promise. Now that both their part of the deal had been met, it was time to go home.

x

The boat we are on is called the Red Peony. A father and his son take care of it and will let us cross with them. Because of the tight space and the presence of cargo and a dozen extra people, we've all settled to sleep on the deck under the stars. Travelling on a narrowboat is nothing compared to sailing at sea: it's calm and peaceful and... does not upset my stomach!

x

As I write these lines, although the sun is playing hide and seek behind grey clouds today, I'm not the only one out: there are otters playing near the riverbank. Their cute, tiny little head lifts up when we cross past them and I can't help the childish awe from settling in. To pass the time, Jack and I try to spot and name as many birds and fish as we can see. Luke, the sailor's son is far better at this game than we are. Kingfishers, sterns, moorhens, geese, ducks or even grebes: he knows them all and can differentiate them before my eyes can catch the difference from afar.

x

We've reached the Bridge of White Towers. According to Luke and his father, we'll reach the capital within the hour. I'm excited to reach Zeryn as I cannot wait to explore every corner. I'm also excited because it means our next and final stop will be Hereward. My journey is nearing its end.

x

There are no words to describe how big, bustling and beautiful this city is. Tomorrow, Jack, who grew up here, will take me to his favourite places.

x

There are different places to see in a capital city. Of course, there are a few obvious choices when Zeryn is the capital city we're talking about. Let's start with the palace for example. No matter where you are in the city, you can catch a glimpse of its tall, white towers, akin to the bridge we crossed to get here - though much taller, of course. Jack woke me up at dawn in order to see them as the sun rose. The light was breathtaking.

Because we woke up so early, breakfast wasn't ready at the inn (the innkeepers were stunned to see us awake so soon after the amount of alcohol some of Tarel's men drank last night) so Jack took me to the bakery he used to visit when he was younger. While we feasted on delicious pastries, Jack shared a lot more about his childhood. He always likes to lie and invent a new life whenever someone asks him about his past. Today, however, I learned the truth. He's an orphan, one who grew up in the streets of the capital. He first crossed paths with Tarel about six years ago, when he was barely fourteen. "I tried to steal in his pocket, and the man rewarded me with a job instead. Crazy man, isn't he? Been on the road with him ever since," Jack confided as he finished eating. If I didn't know any better, I'd say Jack almost got teary-eyed reminiscing.

If he did, however, he didn't let me see any more of it and we ran to our next stop. Jack knows every corner of the city and knows a lot of people too. It seems that while he grew up, he worked for a couple of people in the town districts. I was mesmerised to observe the people hard at work in their workshop. Back home, the only artworks I see are my old sketches on the kitchen wall. Here there are talented craftspeople everywhere I look: swordsmiths turning metal into sharpened blades, glassblowers transforming bubbles of molten glass into pieces akin to jewellery, artists adding intricate details to their work whether their canvas is made out of linen fibres or pristine ceramic. I could watch them for hours.

After the craftspeople district, Jack and I headed toward the arena where people can sometimes spot the Queen's knights training. Sadly for us, they weren't there today. Lucky for us, it meant we got to stand in the middle of the ring, imagining ourselves as the mighty fighters who stood there. I will come back to witness one of those royal tournaments someday.

THE QUEEN'S CHAMPION

LOCATION: CAPITAL CITY OF ZERYN

The comings and goings of townspeople, travellers, and merchants alike usually characterised the streets of Zeryn. The presence of the palace on the higher grounds of town made the capital one of the most secure places in the kingdom. It was a good city to live in and most citizens were always happy to participate in or attend the royal events. Today was one of those days: all had deserted their duties to attend the national tournament and were now standing in the wooden bleachers of the arena, shouting and encouraging their favourite challenger as they watched the succession of duels during the day.

Standing at the centre of the arena, Lenore's ears couldn't miss the deafening blur of the noise, shouts and cheers mixing with the clapping of hands and stomping of feet on the bleachers. Since the start of the tournament, even though she'd been focused on her duels, she hadn't been able to stop herself from smiling because of the good atmosphere radiating from the crowd.

Now, after an entire afternoon of duels and jousts, the tournament was almost over, and, for the third time in a row since she started participating, Lenore was one of the finalists.

The crowd was quiet. Everyone held their breath as she stood before her last opponent, waiting for an opening.

Sir Thomas bore the colours of a neighbouring duchy. She knew him very well and had fought him several times in tournaments similar to this one before. The white and blue coat of arms on his shield was battered and dirty. He'd fought bravely until now, but Lenore knew he couldn't win.

She wouldn't let him.

She didn't even have to reach her limits to defeat him.

Friend or foe, battlefield or tournament, the Scarlet Knight was merciless.

Sword at the ready behind her shield, she observed the way he seemed to put more weight on his left leg. How his breathing was harsher than it was before – a result of a nasty fall earlier, perhaps. The afternoon heat and the weight of his heavier armour probably weren't helping either.

Lenore smiled behind the visor of her helmet.

There it is.

She dropped her shield to the ground and lunged forward, taking him by surprise.

The crowd gasped.

Sir Thomas managed to block her attack but not fast enough to avoid the next blow.

His next parry was too weak, too slow. With a strong and efficient swing, Lenore sent his sword to the ground. Breathless and unarmed, Sir Thomas had no choice but to use his shield as his only defence.

Lenore, freed of the weight of her own, moved faster and took advantage of the slow movements of her weakened opponent. With one last kick to the chest, she knocked him off balance and he crashed to the ground.

The tip of her sword brushed against his gorget in no time.

His hand hit the ground three times.

Cheers erupted from the crowd: The Scarlet Knight was victorious.

Smiling to herself, Lenore sheathed back her sword and helped Sir Thomas back to his feet.

When she turned around, helmet raised high above her head to claim her victory, Queen Maeve II was already smiling down at her, applauding proudly with the rest of the crowd.

Lenore put a hand on her shoulder and bowed before the queen and her husband.

Ever since she had become a royal knight, Lenore had won several tournaments but none could compare to this one. Every year, knights from all over the country travelled to the capital for the Summer Festivities. Whenever Lenore stepped into the arena as the Scarlet Knight, it was to represent Queen Maeve and her colours. For her, it was the greatest honour of all as well as the best occasion to find a worthy opponent.

The queen stood up, regal in her purple summer gown. A rose gold crown of diamonds and amethysts sat on top of her braided hair. She looked magnificent and no one in the crowd would contradict Lenore's mind – especially not the king. As she quickly glanced at him, Lenore hid her smile, seeing the love in King Alexander's eyes.

After years at Maeve's service, Lenore had grown very attached to the royal couple and she was proud to call them her friends.

She would do anything for them.

When the queen raised her hand, the clamour died down almost instantly. Everyone was ready to listen to her.

"People of Zeryn," Maeve started, "once again the Scarlet Knight emerges triumphant from this tournament. Today, we have seen her defeat the most valiant knights of this realm. She is my bravest soldier; a cherished friend of the crown and one last chance remains for you to challenge her. Who will be brave enough to pick up the gauntlet?"

Or stupid enough, Lenore thought, picking up her sword on the ground.

Maeve, as previous rulers before her, always gave that last one call, but no one ever answered it.

No one was crazy enough to do so.

"I will."

Lenore stopped moving. Much like her, the crowd had gone quiet upon hearing the challenger. Surely she misheard. *It couldn't–*

Lenore had yet to turn around and face the challenger, but as she got ready to do so, she caught sight of the royal couple and the surprised, yet pleased smiles both rulers displayed. Childish mischief emanated from the queen's side of the canopy and as her knight-turned-friend finally turned around to face her challenger, the queen winked. When Lenore saw the face of the stranger who'd dared to answer the queen's challenge, she couldn't help but laugh.

Of course, it's him.

A year had gone by since he'd left and this was the moment he chose to show up again? He sure had nailed his entrance for once.

There, barely a few feet away from her, stood Ciarán – a bounty hunter she had had the joy – though bitter at first – to travel and work with a year ago as they both hunted down the same criminal.

She'd been the one to present him with the deal that had led to their temporary partnership. He wouldn't claim his bounty just yet, he would let him go back to his leader, and together they'd uncover the whole organisation. She'd promised him far more gold than the single bounty he was after, knowing full well (or rather, hoping very strongly and confidently) that the queen would accept to reward such achievement. In the end, they had tracked the league of rodents all across the kingdom, had uncovered their stronghold, and brought their leader back to the capital. To this day, the man was still rotting in prison.

As her mind went down memory lane, skipping from the first time they met in a drought alleyway, to moments on the road spent bickering on their horses, minutes before being attacked and having to protect one another, Lenore couldn't help but recall with a bitter taste the way he'd left without a word. Yet, her treacherous heart was happy to see him again and her curiosity was already begging her to start asking questions about his whereabouts, while the grudge she held had yet to let her know how nice she would ask said questions.

Blissfully unaware of her inner monologue and potential threats to his life, Ciarán put a hand to his chest and bowed respectfully towards the royal couple and their guests, never once breaking eye contact with Lenore as he did so.

From where she stood, Lenore could see the proud and smug grin on his face. A true bastard's smile.

Around them, the crowd was buzzing once more. All had turned to their neighbours and friends, wondering who the newcomer was. Wondering who was this stranger bearing no house colours and who no one seemed to be able to recognise, else the queen and the champion herself.

When the queen raised her hand, a sign that she would speak, the crowd immediately ushered its busy gossiping, eager to finally get a potential answer from their ruler about the stranger's identity.

"What a nice surprise. It's been a while since you've last been seen around here. I hope you're enjoying the festivities… Orion."

Upon hearing the alias, the crowd grew loud again. Everyone in town and beyond had heard about Orion. His name was already well known in the lower districts of town, but since his feat with one of the most renowned knights of the kingdom, he had earned a new kind of reputation, even amongst the higher members of society.

Not falling for the queen's fake tone of surprise unlike the rest of the crowd, Lenore eyed her suspiciously. With her attention solely focused on them both, the knight couldn't miss the quick, victorious smile the ruler of Zeryn sent to her husband. Lenore recognised it immediately as the one she always gave him when she'd just won a bet.

She expected him, Lenore realised with a start. *For how long has she known he was in town?*

Maeve owed her a little talk but for now, Lenore didn't have time for those questions. Ciarán was up to something and she was benevolent in erasing that smug smile off of his face.

"I have, your Highness," Ciarán answered. "And I barely just started."

As he finished his sentence, he turned away from the queen only to focus all his attention on Lenore once more. His smug smile stretched further, dark eyes challenging her silently. As he had done moments prior before the queen, he bowed, putting a hand over his heart as he addressed her for the first time since he'd left town without much of a warning, before even claiming his prize.

"I, Orion, humble bounty hunter as I am, challenge you to a

duel… Scarlet."

For a second, he almost had her believe he'd call her by her true name in front of everyone. When he doesn't, the reminder that he knew what many didn't, sent a shiver down her spine. She pushed back the thought and every other feeling the sight of him awakened in her and unsheathed her sword.

Wild cheers erupted from the crowd at the sight.

At the same time, Maeve raised both her arms. "Let the battle begin!"

Ciarán didn't need to wait for the queen's permission or the cheers of the crowd to lunge forward. His two swords struck Lenore's blade with a clashing sound.

Lenore smiled. The tournament had just gotten a hundred times more interesting.

"Missed me much, darling?" He asked, his voice still as playful as the last time she saw him.

If she didn't know any better, she'd say he was flirting with her.

"Obviously."

She knew her answer wasn't entirely ironic but he didn't need to know that. She pushed back against his swords. He jumped backwards, avoiding her attacks.

"Where have you been all this time?"

Their swords clashed again.

"Wouldn't you like to know…"

Wherever he'd been, he hadn't skimped on his training. His armour, lighter than the one Lenore was wearing, allowed him more freedom of movement. He knew perfectly how to wield both of his swords at a time or to use their height difference as an advantage. His moves were swifter than ever, brutal and efficient. His technique, opposite to what every knight was taught, kept Lenore on her toes, never letting her guard down in order not to fall for any of his dirty tricks.

He was anything but a knight.

And it was exactly what had always made him a very interesting sparring partner for Lenore.

No matter how skilled he might be, however, he wasn't the only one who'd been training. She'd fought her share of bandits when she was on the road with him and had learned even more tricks with the royal soldiers in the past year. She wouldn't back down from a challenge so easily.

Even less so when she had unfinished business and scores to settle with her opponent.

She swung her sword around, aiming for his shoulders, his legs, his arms and back to his face again. And he did just the same to her. They moved around the arena in a deadly dance, switching attacks and techniques every second. Their strategy evolved almost as fast as they parried each other's moves.

Ciarán crossed his swords and blocked Lenore's right above his knee.

She smiled to herself.

Exactly what she'd been looking for.

Thanks, Love.

If he had his two hands occupied, it wasn't her case. Protected by her gauntlet, she reached for his sword with her left hand and stole it from his grasp.

Barely showing any sign of surprise, he blocked her next attack almost too easily.

He knew she'd managed to do that at some point, Lenore realised. He'd prepared himself for it.

Maybe she hadn't been the only one reminiscing about their past combats and the strategy the other had used to win against opponents.

Not allowing herself to be destabilised over a single failed trick, she ran toward him once more.

Before reaching him, however, she dropped the second sword in the sand and kicked it far away with her left foot.

"I'm not stupid," she said, looking him in the eye as their swords clashed once more.

Ciarán never wore a helmet to battle. While hers was still in the sand, discarded by the royal's podium since the end of her fight with Sir Thomas, Ciarán preferred to walk into battle with as little restriction as possible. According to the explanations he'd given her one night as they sat to drink, helmets, as life-saving as they might be, were too heavy for his taste and restricted both his vision and movement too much. At the time, she'd theorised it was mostly because it kept him from taunting his opponents with the snarky comments he loved to make, and he'd laughed, agreeing with her before downing his drink and leaving for the night.

Today was no different. His face was as bare as always, allowing every shift of his expression to be read by her. And, there, as their faces stood inches apart, Lenore caught a glint of surprise amidst his unreadable expression. Somehow, he hadn't seen that move coming.

Yet, it would have been a foolish move to keep that sword.

Foolish and as arrogant as possible. She wasn't used to fighting with two swords, and hers was too heavy to be handled with a twin. It would have slowed her down, inevitably granting more room for weaknesses and mistakes on her part.

She didn't intend to let him win so easily.

They kept on blocking each other blows, making it almost impossible to know who had the upper hand. But when shielding herself from one of his latest attacks, Lenore made the mistake of forgetting an important detail in the heat of the moment.

Her hair, usually kept from people's reach by her helmet, was now exposed since her last duel.

Ciarán didn't hesitate one second and grabbed her braid with his now free hand.

Pain shot to her scalp and she hissed.

Unfazed, he only teased her further. "Not stupid, huh?"

Lenore grunted and glared at him. "You wanna play dirty? Fine. Let's play dirty."

She slammed her elbow in his jaw and shot her leg backwards. His male primary instincts taking over, he jumped backwards to protect himself and let go of her braid.

Lenore took that opportunity to put some distance between the two of them and slid her braid inside her armour. She wouldn't make the same mistake twice.

Ciarán spat on the ground. "Not bad," he said, snapping his jaw. She hated that sound. "But I think you're getting rusty."

"Am I?"

"Let me prove it to you."

He lunged forward, moving faster than he was before if that's even possible. When Lenore barely managed to counterattack his next move, she realised what was wrong. He wasn't moving faster. She was the one moving slower. After a whole afternoon spent fighting, her limbs were becoming heavy, and her wrists ached.

Even she had her limits, and she would reach them soon.

"Getting a little tired, aren't you?"

"You wish!"

Rage, annoyance or pure spite, she didn't know what fuelled her energy anymore. With a surge of renewed stamina, she charged and slammed her shoulders in his chest. His armour took the brunt of the hit but he lost his sword in the process and hit the wall behind him.

They were just below the royal platform, Lenore realised, once again aware of her surroundings. The cheers of the crowd came back to her and for one split second, she thought she finally had the advantage once and for all. She even saw Maeve winking at her.

But even pinned to the wall and stripped of both his weapons, Ciarán wouldn't back down. Lenore would pay the price of her carelessness. While she allowed herself to get distracted for a second by the crowd and Maeve, he used that opportunity to kick her leg and flip her under him.

Air was knocked out of her lungs as they both hit the ground this time.

Ciarán sat on top of her, pinning her down.

The sun was blinding her but she didn't need to see to be aware of her surroundings now. If they were near the royal seats, then she had one last weapon to use against him.

She stretched her arm in the sand and before he could understand what she intended on doing, she threw her abandoned helmet at his face.

Right in the bull's eye.

Or rather, right onto his nose.

She didn't gloat much longer, however, and got back on her feet. She ran toward the centre of the arena where her shield was waiting for her. A bold red dot against the sand.

She reached it just in time to yield it and stop Ciarán's next attack. The sword she'd ditched for him earlier was now back in his hand, slamming against her shield with every of her parry.

Without the adrenaline of a real, life-threatening situation to keep them moving, her muscles were too tired to keep up with this rhythm for long. With one last feint, Ciarán managed to move faster than she'd predicted. He brandished his sword and, using all of his strength, let it fall back on her shield. This time, her arm gave in and her shield hit the sand.

They both stood still, breathless and bruised.

His elbow was bent in front of his eyes, the tip of his sword against her panting throat.

For a fleeting moment, the crowd remained silent.

While they processed what she already knew, Lenore stared at Ciarán. She definitely hadn't gone easy on him. His nose was bleeding. So was his eyebrow arch and there was a nasty bruise already blooming on his jaw from the punch she'd landed on his chin earlier. Yet, he was smiling, almost laughing as he too, observed her from the other side of his blade.

"I missed you too," he finally said.

Then, he lowered his weapon and the crowd erupted.

Now they knew it too.

The fight was over.

And the Champion had lost.

After a whole day spent sightseeing and wishing I had all the money in the world to buy everything I set my eyes on, I settled on a few souvenirs. As we crossed one of the many small bridges in the city centre, I bought a tiny oil painting from a woman by the river and a book on the history of the royal family from the man who kept the shop right next to her. Because Ella insisted that I bought souvenirs for the family, I picked a watercolour drawing depicting the palace at sunrise for Ella, a bracelet for mom and a carved knife for dad.

Jack promised to hand them their little gifts in person when he travels back to Beryl and then Greenblades with Tarel's group. He's also promised to send me letters. Once I have my new address, I've been asked to send a letter to the guard post at the bridge of White Towers. According to Jack's saying: "I'm friend with the guards, they'll keep my letters safe!" (When I asked how he became friends with them, he simply answered that they were the ones who taught him how to play cards. After their shift, I hope...)

Today was a long day, but as I write these lines in bed (while praying my candle lasts till I finish my last sentence) and put today's adventures to paper, committing them to memory, I feel grateful to be travelling with Jack and Tarel. No day is a boring day with such travelling companions.

x

Tarel had warned us that we would not stay long in the capital (unfortunately). Therefore, today, it's time to wake up at dawn. Again. Destination? Hereward.

x

I'm the only traveller who remains from Tarel's first stops on the western roads. Now, others have joined us. Our merry little group is ready for departure! This time around, my horse is a white stallion named Snow. He doesn't seem to be a prankster like Zephyr. Calmer, too. Me, however? I'm restless at the thought that soon, Hereward will be in sight.

x

While we set up camp for the night, I found a card left by Jack. It sounds like a goodbye already, even though we have a week ahead of us before it's time to say our actual goodbyes.

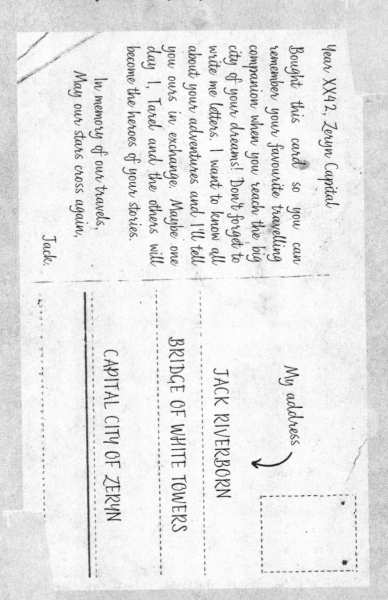

Year XX42, Zeryn Capital

Bought this card so you can remember your favourite travelling companion when you reach the big city of your dreams! Don't forget to write me letters. I want to know all about your adventures and I'll tell you ours in exchange. Maybe one day 1, Tarel and the others will become the heroes of your stories.

In memory of our travels,
May our stars cross again,

Jack.

My address →

JACK RIVERBORN

BRIDGE OF WHITE TOWERS

CAPITAL CITY OF ZERYN

As if I'd forget the adventures of the past month! Never!

Though it's true that, much like Jack, I can't help but wonder when will be the next time I see them all again. I will miss them a lot.

GENTLE SUNLIGHT

As morning came to replace the moon and stars, the horizon lit up with colours. Progressively, the sky faded from pure darkness to warm shades of bright reds and bold yellows.

As the sky put on its daylight attire, the world underneath shifted in sync. Grasslands and wheat fields, painted in shivering shadows moments prior, came back to life in luscious touches of greens and golds.

Then, the dawn brought from the dark the silhouettes of sleeping homes, basking them in gentle sunlight, before ending its course in the stained-glass windows of the castle at the top of the hill.

A ROYAL COMMISSION

The swordsmith's gloved fingers grazed the sharp blade with cautious excitement. After months of hard work, the sword, now gleaming under the warm, red light of the hearth, was finally ready.

As he observed the final result, looking for any default he might have missed, the swordsmith knew that each weapon he'd forged before, paled in comparison. Commissioned by the queen herself and made of the finest components of all Three Realms, the sword already stood out as his greatest accomplishment.

Patriotic pride coursed his veins at the thought that, soon, the kingdom's greatest knight would brandish it to battle.

MOLTEN GLASS

Slowly, carefully, the glass-maker turned the metal blowpipe into the clay mould and blew air in the hot, liquid glass. Immediately, the transparent material started to melt, taking shape with every breath and flick of the craftsman's wrist.

Then, the man cautiously opened the mould and picked up his other tools to twist and shape the molten glass into a colourful vase.

Hours later, once his newest creation had cooled down, he came back, smile on his face, gold paint in hand, and applied the finishing touch with as much care and caution he had shown during the previous steps.

IN THE SPOTLIGHT

She twirled and twirled onstage. Her red dress flew with every spin, showing her legs and polished heels. Never missing a step, she made a partner out of the notes filling up the room, drawing all attention to herself.

Her smile grew bigger.

Under the eyes of drunk old men or fancy noblewomen, the stage was the same. From the picturesque opera house to the notorious cabaret, she would dance all day and all night long for that was where she truly belonged.

Whenever she danced, she felt as if she was touching the sky, jumping from star to star.

In four days, we will reach the outskirts of Hereward. For now, we travel on the roads under merciful skies. Since the last storm on the Demarion, we haven't seen a cloud of rain since we reached the east coasts. Everyone prays it stays that way as it's more enjoyable to travel while listening to the song of crickets and cicadas or exchanging jokes with others than it is enduring heavy rainfalls while riding horseback for hours.

x

Knowing it's my last couple of days with everyone, I try to enjoy every second of it. During the day, I talk to everyone, asking them to tell me more of the stories or to start telling them once more if they have no more. I want to remember everything. By now, everyone is used to my "thirst for stories", as Tarel likes to call it. If they have the right to never get tired of the same tasteless ale, I get to enjoy listening to stories, don't I? I need them. At night, I've been writing letters to send to my family once I reach Hereward. I want to tell them about everything that happened, everything that I learned about everywhere and everyone as if they'd been there along with me. I know Ella would approve.

I decided to send one of these letters to Izzy as well (along with the finished first draft of the story she started to read when I was in Beryl). She was my very first friend on the road, I hope she will like to hear more of my adventures, even if I'm not here to pay her 'one last ale' in the style of the sailors she usually listens to every night.

x

There's not a lot to say about the journey so far. Everything is going according to plan. I think I'm going more impatient to reach our destination and my restless thoughts can't find the time to write anymore.

x

After three days of travelling with our convoy, we will finally reach Hereward tomorrow. We've set up camp in a forest. Tomorrow, I will see for the first time the High Ruins that precede anyone's arrival in the city.

x

When I was little, grandpa was the first to teach me about the legends of our Kingdom. One of the first stories that I remember, and one that everyone knows in the country, is the legend behind the High Ruins of Hereward. Walls with heights akin to the tallest trees of the Emerald Sea, so high writers of Ancient Times often compared them to a small mountain range. The high wall was built in a circle around the perimeter of Hereward, ten miles away from the city - protection inherited from when Hereward was a Kingdom of its own. Though the fortification now bears the name of fallen bricks, it looks nothing like ruins. It still withstands the passing of time, protected by the knowledge and magic of the creatures that once protected the land and built those walls: dragons.

x

"As humans rose and gathered, as land became home to them,
Dragons gave up their caves and clouds
and left the Realms.

In their wake, a single gift remained for the new tenants of the World.
Forever standing, the high walls of the last dragon king's palace
would stand still and keep the peace at its heart.

There, a new nation would prevail."

x

After crossing the High Ruins, Hereward opened its arms to us. After weeks of travel, after countless hours spent on a saddle or the deck of a ship, I had finally reached my final destination. When I first saw the city, emotion caught my throat. I dreamed about that day so many times and now... Now it was finally happening. Soon, I would cross the city gates and soon my steps would lead me to the wrought-iron gates of the Academy. Soon, I would officially become an Elite Apprentice. Finally. Jack (along with everyone else) has yet to stop teasing me about my excitement. However, he understands what it means for me. I can't wait to explore the city. I want to see as much as I can before the sunset!

x

The city of Hereward, home to the prestigious Academy at its centre, is one of the biggest cities in the Kingdom, second only to the capital city. As we travelled the land, Tarel told me more about it. Hereward is always bustling with life, with only a few hours of quiet during the night where silence replaces the chaos and loud hustle of both day activities and night parties. In those late hours, only the sound of the patrolling squadron's boots would break the peace and quiet of the night. Sitting on a bench, after spending my day and most of the night exploring said streets, I can already tell he wasn't lying. Even if there are no specific festivals in town today, I've never seen such positive energy in a town's streets before. Even if the cities and ports I visited on my way here were just as busy, there's something different here. Jack says I'm biased. He might be right.

This morning, after we crossed the gates of the city, our group split for the day. Even if we reached Hereward, I'm still under Tarel's care until tomorrow after I attend the graduation ceremony of the current Elite Students. Open to the public, many of the city residents attend.

First, Jack and I headed toward the market plaza where we got to try several pastries and local dishes. Compared to Zeryn's capital where dishes often involve fresh fish from the river, here, bakers and cooks take advantage of the proximity of the region's best orchards. Everything looks and tastes marvellous, leaving you to want more. Before Jack and I spent our whole allowance on treats, we headed toward the other districts to explore. While we visited the city, we stopped to admire a beautiful mural painted on one of the city walls. Painted in bright colours and intricate details, it depicted the legend of the city's birth: from when the land still belonged to the Ancient Dragons to where it stands now, home of our people & history. I hope to learn more about this legend at the Academy.

While I kept looking around everywhere, not wanting to miss a single bit about my new city, Jack spent every moment petting every stray cat that crossed our path. He still regrets not having been able to take Black with him. If this goes on, Tarel will have to watch out for a stowaway furball amongst his ranks...

Today is the big day. Today, I'll cross the iron gates of the prestigious Academy of Hereward for the first time. It's just as exciting and magical, and as it is terrifying and overwhelming to think about. I'm nervous, both from anxiety and excitement. I waited years. The day is finally here.

x

The graduation ceremony starts late in the morning and ends around noon. After a good breakfast, I decided to go for a walk in the city, this time on my own. After finishing my last letters, I headed toward the Academy early. Even before crossing the gates, one can smell in the air the perfume of flowers mixing with the one of herbal medicine coming from the gardens. As I walked, I crossed paths with several students. I think I saw a few of them yesterday when I was sightseeing with Jack. Elite Students are easy to spot: with their uniforms, they stand out in crowds. On this special day, however, their recognisable black robes are embroidered with threads of reds and golds, colours of the Hereward's coat of arms. On their chest, the medal symbolising their fifth year shines on their shirt. All of them chat excitedly, talking about the upcoming ceremony and the big decision they'll take today: each of them must choose the order they'll follow, which will then determine the last years of their apprenticeship. While some will choose the orders of the Knights, others aim to become doctors and scientists, while the remaining students will choose to become the guardians of the Realms' past, present and future as Elite Historians. Later that morning, after listening to several speeches from their headmistress and teachers, I, alongside Tarel's troops and Hereward's citizens, was a witness of their choice.

x

As the whole town celebrates after the ceremony, my last night with Tarel, Jack and the others, starts. Tomorrow, they'll depart and a new chapter will start for all of us. As I wait for them to come down, my pen writes a new story inspired by the students I met today. I hope writing about them won't be a bad omen for my future. As I reminisce about their graduation, I can't help but wonder what my first day at the Academy will be like... One thing remains sure, however: tonight, Tarel pays the bill!

x

YOUR DESTINY BEGINS

LOCATION: THE ACADEMY OF HEREWARD

When the sun rose about the city of Hereward, Kalya was still downtown. It wasn't the first time the student had found herself alone in the early hours of the day, wandering around the city. Unable to sleep, she'd spent the night exploring the streets and strolling on the city ramparts. Now sitting on the roof of the Rising Sun — the most popular tavern in the city and her favourite hiding spot — she took pleasure in observing the city as it woke up along with the sun.

Across from her, the plaza was growing busier by the minute as merchants were preparing their stalls for the market. It was barely four in the morning, and the first customers wouldn't arrive before another two hours, but the comings and goings of all sorts of merchants had already started. Only twenty minutes ago the plaza had been empty. Now around fifteen tents had already been set up.

They reminded Kalya of ants and bees – all working hard on their tasks and knowing exactly what they were meant to do, starting their routine every day like clockwork.

Kalya liked to observe them from afar. Whenever she was stressed or worried, it calmed her down to sit down and simply observe other people go about their day and to witness once more the routines she'd seen multiple times already. It grounded her in the present, reminding her that the world was still functioning normally and that her worries were only temporary: soon, everything would be alright, routine-like again for her too.

And when it came to schedules and routines, merchants from the plaza were her favourite people to observe for they were the most predictable people she knew.

Every day without fail, they would arrive around four and start to get ready before their first customers arrived. Fishmongers and market gardeners usually arrived first, then came the cattle sellers – Kalya loved how everything grew immediately louder as soon as they and their animals entered the plaza. The last stalls to be set up were kept by all sorts of merchants and craftspeople. From food and drinks to houseware or even small weapons like daggers, one could find everything at the marketplace.

Within two hours, everything would be set up and merchants would all be ready to meet the request of their first buyers. Buyers whose routine Kalya knew just as well: servants often came before all merchants were ready, shopkeepers from the shopping district would come before opening their own shop, and then around six, the first citizens and visitors would come – which was right after the Night Watch was relieved, and the city gates were opened. Then, at around six in the afternoon, merchants would undo their stalls, leave the plaza, and the temporary wooden stage of a troop of dancers or comedians would replace them, and the bustling sound of a partying crowd would replace the negotiations and trades of the day.

Kalya took pride in knowing her city and its people so well. She knew its layout and organisation like the back of her hand and would never grow tired of observing it, no matter the time of the day or night.

The mouth-watering smell of food coming from the plaza woke Kalya's appetite. She stood up from her spot on the rooftop, climbed down the walls she'd escalated hours prior, and headed straight toward the plaza, hoping to get a few treats from the merchants before she'd have to go back to the Academy. She wouldn't be able to run from her responsibilities for much longer. Kalya was no merchant; she was an apprentice at the Academy of Hereward – heart of the city and jewel of the kingdom – and today was the day of her graduation.

Ignoring the thumping of her heart and the worries of her stressed-out mind, she made her way through the different stalls and only stopped when she reached one in the middle of the plaza, near her favourite spot by the fountain: the baker's stall. When she arrived, Kalya was welcomed by the sight of different sorts of freshly-baked loaves of bread, brioches and pastries which only made her stomach growl even more.

Elijah and his father were both standing behind the delicious display, a warm smile on their face. Her excitement at the sight of their baked goods never failed to make them smile and they would often tease her about never being able to choose which pastry she wanted to taste first. She and Elijah would often joke about her ability to be so determined and set on a choice that would determine the course of her whole life, yet be irremediably indecisive on something as simple as a pastry that she could – and would – come back to eat the next day.

Elijah's eyes settled on the uniform she was wearing: the black robes and red embroideries on the hem of her long sleeves were proof of her apprenticeship and all students wore them. The medal on her chest, however, was only earned by students at the end of their fifth year at the Academy, days only before the graduation ceremony. Days only before they were meant to choose their path, a decision that would impact the remaining three years of their Elite Training, and ultimately, the rest of their life.

Both bakers knew today was no ordinary day.

She wondered if they could read the nerves on her face.

"Morning, Kalya," Elijah's father greeted. "Wandering the streets again?"

Kalya crossed her arms behind her back and nodded. "You know I can't help it. Had to see the city one last time before the ceremony."

"You say that as if you're going to leave forever," Elijah said. "It's only graduation, Kalya. The city will be the same tomorrow, as well as the day after. You'll be okay."

"Thanks, El'. I know I'm probably stressed for nothing…"

"It's a big change for you, it's normal to be a little nervous," Elijah's father said from behind the stacks of pastries. His warm voice was as comforting as the pastries he made. "But you'll be okay, Kalya. Don't worry about it."

"And we'll be rooting for you from here!" Elijah said as he handed her one of her favourite treats: a small brioche filled with strawberry jam and sprinkled with flour sugar – a true delight. "It's on the house," he added with a wink.

Kalya frowned. "You've never let me have stuff for free before."

"What can I say," he smiled, "today is a special day. And besides, I couldn't possibly have let you get used to special treatment. But you can't blame me for being friendly with Miss Future Elite now, can you?"

Kalya scoffed and bit into the warm dough. The taste of butter instantly calmed her thumping heart and she relished the sweet taste of jam hitting her taste buds as her teeth reached the middle of the brioche. As usual, Elijah's baked goods were the best.

"Thanks for the food, you two. I'll see you tomorrow!"

"Don't worry. Same place, same time."

Despite the baker and his son's protest, Kalya dropped three coins on the wooden table and ran off toward the city centre and the wrought-iron gates of the Academy.

*

Much like the other parts of the city, the Academy had started to wake. If Kalya didn't want to be late on such a special day, she'd have to hurry. Even if today was no ordinary day on campus, it wouldn't mean teachers would be more relaxed on discipline and punctuality. She couldn't allow herself to be caught late on such an important day. She wouldn't risk being refused attendance at the ceremony.

She ran across town, barely phased anymore by the steeped cobbled streets and confusing labyrinth of the city's layout that left tourists both disoriented and short of breath. The city of Hereward was built around a hill with the Academy standing at the very top, overlooking the city and the grasslands that stretched all around it. Once a stronghold during century-old wars, the fortified city of Hereward was now mostly known for being a major crossroad of trading routes and the host of the Elite Academy, where the most renowned Scholars, Knights and Healers of the Kingdom of Zeryn did their apprenticeship.

After crossing the wrought-iron gates and greeting the guards, Kalya headed straight for the rose garden on the left of the main building. Instead of running toward the pristine staircase of the main entrance – which would inevitably mean crossing paths with teachers and having to explain why she was coming from outside and not the dorms – she took the shortcut by the rose garden, ran past the greenhouse and its medicinal plants and entered the corridor to the dining hall from one of the doors that led to the inner courtyard of the ancient fortress. When she reached the hallway, the breakfast bell had yet to reach its last toll.

Even if she wasn't exactly late, it didn't stop Kalya from being met by the judgmental, tired glare of Lizzie – her best friend and roommate ever since they entered the Academy – from the other side of the hallway. Feigning innocence, Kalya strolled toward her and greeted her as the other students walked past them to enter the dining hall.

"You ran off again," Lizzie scolded, arms crossed on her chest.

"I don't know what you're talking about, Lizzie."

"You're wearing the same shirt as yesterday; your cloak is crinkled in the back and you weren't there when I woke up this morning."

"Fine, you win," Kalya sighed, not even trying to defend herself. "I was in town. I went to the shopping district and stopped by the market."

Kalya knew it was pointless to try and hide it. If she wasn't studying to become a healer, Lizzie would have made a fine detective. In the five years they'd shared at the Academy, Kalya had often been the prey of Lizzie's observant eyes and analytical skills. No matter how stealthy Kalya had grown to be, Lizzie would always know about her secret adventures before Kalya would even think about spilling the beans to her. During their first year, they'd become best friends on the night Lizzie had stopped her from being caught by the headmistress, which would have inevitably led to her expulsion. Four years later, Kalya had yet to stop her night excursions – much to Lizzie's displeasure.

In front of her, Lizzie clicked her tongue, playing with the end of her blond curls like she would whenever she didn't know whether to keep being mad (though she was never truly angry, simply "worried to death", as she would say herself) or to drop the case. "Today is our big day. You could have been caught and ruined everything for yourself."

"It's because it's our big day that I had to get out. Was too stressed out, and needed to get some air. Besides, it's not like the headmistress would know."

Lizzie sighed and threw her hair back. "You're going to be the end of me someday, you know. Couldn't even spare my heart on our last day, could you?"

Knowing her friend had decided to drop the case, Kalya wrapped her arm around Lizzie's shoulder with a victorious smile and led her inside the dining hall, now loud and filled with starving students. From their first year to their fifth, all students were expected to be here for breakfast. Then for the remaining three years of their destined apprenticeship, eating in the main hall was no longer mandatory for the three departments had their own designated wings and common rooms. Today, the large room was busier than ever, and not even the priestesses managed to quiet the excited murmur in the room. Kalya even suspected them to be as excited about today's event as the students were and to be more lenient than usual – which couldn't hurt for once.

"Look, I'm just in time for breakfast. Chill out, Liz."

"If you were out and about, you could have at least brought me back some treats from Elijah's," Lizzie grumbled. "We both know anything he does is way better than anything we could eat here."

"We can go grab them later."

"They're better in the morning and you know it," Lizzie pouted.

"Then I guess you'll have to come on an escapade with me next time."

"No! Forget I said anything, don't you dare wake me up, I'm good. I care about my sleep schedule, unlike some people."

Kalya laughed and stopped to sit at the table assigned to their class. Lizzie had worried for nothing; they weren't even the last ones from their class to arrive.

"Come on, time for our last breakfast here. Soon we can say goodbye to Mr Sermon's horrible cooking."

Lizzie huffed a laugh and both girls started to eat. As always, breakfast time lingered, kept alive by conversations with their classmates about the food the cooks from the other departments would make them, the new classes they would have and the outfits they'd wear during the graduation ceremony. Some were already placing bets on the length of the headmistress's speech and whether or not she would cry, overwhelmed by the emotion of her "unruly flock of chicks barely out of their eggshell", finally taking their biggest step toward flying out of the nest.

Distracted by the delightful mood and the warm food in her stomach, Kalya managed to forget about her nerves for a moment and enjoyed her meal with her friends, trying to commit everything to memory.

*

Three hours later, students of all years were gathered again, in the Great Hall this time. Sunlight streamed through the high stained-glass windows, basking students, teachers and close family members in warm, colourful light. From the podium in front of them, the headmistress looked at each apprentice with pride in her eyes. She seemed as impatient as anyone to know which paths each of the apprentices would choose.

Sitting amongst her peers, Kalya met her gaze and kept her head held high. The ceremony was about to begin.

As planned, the graduation ceremony started with a speech from the headmistress which she tried – and failed – to keep short. After five years, all graduates were used to it and found themselves not minding much. Kalya didn't even see the smug, winning smile on most people who had bet against her ability to keep it short and who had therefore won a month worth of chores done by their peers. All of them were slowly realising that, even though they were not going to leave the Academy just yet, everything was about to change and it was the last day they would spend together. Within an hour's time, most attendees had grown just as nostalgic as the headmistress herself. Across the room, Kalya could see a few of her classmates get teary-eyed while others displayed proud smiles on their faces which only hid further emotion.

Once the headmistress had finished her speech, a herald started to call apprentices by their names one by one. When he called for her, Kalya stood up and did the same as others – both her classmates and their alumni before them – had done before.

First, Kalya stepped toward the altar and stopped in front of the headmistress who smiled proudly at her as she handed her diploma over. Then, the older woman extended her arm toward the table next to her. There, three staves representing each Order had been laid out. Each staff was about a metre long and had a distinctive stone sitting at the top. Red for the Order of the Knights, in charge of protecting the city and the kingdom and its citizens. Purple for the Order of Scholars, in charge of protecting the past, present and future by studying, writing and sharing the history of the Realms. Green for the Order of the Healers, in charge of studying the different Sciences and curing citizens of known diseases. Each Order formed the Elites of the Kingdom and all students who graduated from the Academy of Hereward were highly respected throughout the kingdom.

Kalya did not ponder. Her choice had been made long ago. While Lizzie had chosen the green gem barely minutes before her, Kalya picked the red one without hesitating. For a second, she twirled the ornamented staff of the Order of the Knight, admiring it as the red orb caught the late morning sunlight. Then she turned around to face the headmistress once more.

The woman's proud yet nostalgic smile had been replaced by a knowing one as if she'd been expecting such a choice from her student. As Kalya couldn't keep herself from wondering if teachers had betting pools of their own, the headmistress put a firm, comforting hand on her shoulder, silently guiding her toward the other apprentices who had picked the same calling as her.

Playing with the weight of the staff in her hand, Kalya stepped down from the podium while the herald called for someone else. With a proud smile, almost bouncing on her feet, she headed toward the seats where her new comrades were waiting for her.

Kalya didn't know what the world held in store for her, yet she could remind herself of things she knew for sure. Tomorrow, the sun would rise, merchants would install their stalls on the plaza, Elijah and his father would bake more finger-licking delicious pastries, and her new life would begin: tomorrow, she would become the guardian she'd always aspired to be.

My journey and these pages have reached their end. This morning, I said goodbyes to Jack, Tarel and everyone else. Jack promised to pay me a visit and feed me with all sorts of stories when we meet again. Though most of them pray for a safe journey, Jack keeps wishing for more adventure and chaos. According to him, the trip from Beryl to Hereward was too calm. However, he's excited to travel all the way to Greenblades. It'll be his first time seeing the Emerald Sea from up close. I wonder if he'll be brave enough and attempt to see the Guardian. Who knows, he might even see him if he's lucky... As for Tarel, he's taken the last letter I've written for my parents and will deliver it in person to them.

I saw their departure, perched on the high walls of my new city. Farewell, my friends. May the stars protect you on your travels. Soon, new journeys will start for all of us. Until we meet again...

x

Dear notebook, you waited for two years before I put down my first adventures on your pages. Today, I ask that you wait again. The next time I will write on these pages, will be the day of my graduation.

x

Year XX50

It's been eight years. Dear past self... we did it! It's been a long, exhausting journey. Sometimes rewarding, sometimes discouraging, but we did it. We've finally graduated from the Academy. It's official now. I am an Academician of Hereward. Tomorrow, I'll embark on a new journey: one beyond the border of Zeryn - and guess what? Jack is one of the cartographers tagging along! It's a small world! Here's to more adventures and stories! Dear stars, I will be under your protection.

Jorka, Elite Historian, graduate of the Hereward Academy.

LIST OF FEATURED STORIES

ACKNOWLEDGEMENTS

This is it. I'm officially a mother of two! After publishing *Mini Worlds*, I wanted to write a collection of short stories inspired by some of the drabbles I'd written over the years. The fantasy lover that I am could not resist making a collection based on this theme: this is how the idea for *The Wanderer* was born. The four short stories featured in this book were inspired by some of said drabbles as well as my love and need to write about dragons, knights and pirates.

Now that this book is finally out in the world and about to join other stories on shelves, I'd like to thank the people who helped me complete Jorka's journey.

First, Margot and Salomé, college friends turned beta-readers on this project. Thank you for your multiple rereads, insights, comments and encouragements. Without you, this book would still be tagged as a "Work in Progress" in my files.

Then, Maggie. I know that when you'll read these lines you'll think you haven't done anything worthy of being featured on this page but yes you did. Thank you for your endless support, your GIF hype and your heartfelt encouragements since day one. You're the best and deserve all the Oreos in the world.

Honourable mentions go to Jen & Angie: thank you for your live reactions on the book covers. You were amongst the first to see it and confirm it was the right choice. Feeling grateful for all your love.

Finally, Jijii. Lieutenant to my captain, writing buddy and fulltime anxiety shield, thank you for not letting me drop this project. Here's to another "I told you so" on the list.

I could not end these acknowledgements without thanking you, dear reader. Thank you for buying my book and reading my work. I hope you enjoyed this journey and that you'll consider following me on the next one. Until then... *« Bonne lecture ! »*

BY THE SAME AUTHOR:

Mini Worlds, a collection of 100 words stories
by Maud Lelarge, published November 2021 (Amazon KDP)

MINI WORLDS

May 2020, Leeds. Maud is on her way to work when she starts imagining a child, sitting in the grass in front of the houses she passes by, and what could run through her mind. Later that day, the first 100 words story is born.

Many more prompts have followed since then, becoming the playground of Maud's creativity. Set in different worlds and genres, thirty of her drabbles are brought together in this collection, featuring different sets of characters and their stories:

A runaway prince amongst pirates,

A dragon, prisoner of his chains,

A dancer who thrives in the spotlight.

And many more to be discovered...

What do readers say about Mini Worlds?

"This book is very special to me, makes me travel, dream and cry in such a short time span. **Mini Worlds** *is a collection of short stories of 100 words. One might think 100 words is too little for a story, but trust me, Maud Lelarge paints them so beautifully you can see the images clearly in your head and more importantly feel the emotions deep in your heart."* – Demetra M. on Goodreads.

"In **Mini Worlds***, you get emerged into many different, unique worlds and follow diverse characters."* – Lauryn, on Instagram.

"The mini prompts are so well written and so sweet that you can't help but want more out of the stories, they hook you in just right!" – Amazon customer.

FREE DRABBLES & MORE ON INSTAGRAM:

INKTOBER DAY #05
Children of the Isle

Bedtime stories warn children about the witches in the woods who eat the misbehaved ones. But who warns witches about the monsters lurking in their own shadows? No one.

And tonight, another has fallen.

But what could she have done, alone and powerless, against five of those monsters? After all, witches aren't used to play the part of the prey.

Sole witness to the scene, a lonesome raven is the only one able to spread the tale. However, few are the witches willing to believe the story of the Isle of Karmeda - where children are the one eating witches for breakfast.

- MAUD'S 100 WORDS STORIES -
@maudsdrabbles / 05.10.21 / word prompt : raven

Maud shares new word-prompt-inspired drabbles every week and regularly shares about her upcoming book projects on her Instagram account:

@MAUDSDRABBLES

Did you like what you read?
Leave a review online so more people
can discover and read these stories!

FLASH ME!
One QR code for all important links:
Amazon, Goodreads, Instagram…

Thank you for reading!

Printed by Amazon Italia Logistica S.r.l.
Torrazza Piemonte (TO), Italy

56239042R00060